CK

william morrow and company
new york

"It's bedtime," says Mrs. Bear.
"Where are those Busy Bears?"

2268912

"It's bedtime," says Mr. Bear.
"Look at this mess!"

"Brush your teeth,"
says Mrs. Bear.

1 ONE Busy Bear does not hear.
She is having a party.

"Pick up your toys,"
says Mr. Bear.

2

TWO Busy Bears are riding
in their bus.

 "Wash your face and hands," says Mrs. Bear.

3 THREE Busy Bears are splashing in their pool.

"Clean up your room,"
says Mr. Bear.

4

FOUR Busy Bears are working
in their little store.

"Finish your drinks,"
calls Mrs. Bear.

5 FIVE Busy Bears are playing doctors and nurses.

WITCH MAGAZINE

BROOM CUPBOARD

MAGIC

Bright Spells

SPOOK BOOK

SORCE

"Brush your hair,"
calls Mrs. Bear.

6 SIX Busy Bears are making up magic spells.

"Pick up your books,"
calls Mr. Bear.

7 SEVEN Busy Bears are learning numbers.

"Put on your pajamas!"
calls Mrs. Bear.

8 EIGHT Busy Bears are flying to the moon.

"Finish your games!"
says Mr. Bear.

9 NINE Busy Bears shout out, "No! We want to play—one, two, three, go!"

 "Time for a snack," calls Mrs. Bear.
Now look how many bears there are!

10 One, two, three, four, five, six, seven, eight, nine, ten!

TEN sleepy bears say good night!

First published in Great Britain in 1985 by Methuen Children's Books, Ltd., 11 New Fetter Lane, London EC4P 4EE.
All rights reserved. Inquiries should be addressed to William Morrow and Company, Inc., 105 Madison Avenue, New York, N.Y. 10016.
Printed in Great Britain
1 2 3 4 5 6 7 8 9 10
Library of Congress Cataloging in Publication Data
Killingback, Julia.   One, two, three, go! 1. Children's stories, American. [1. Bedtime—Fiction. 2. Bears—Fiction. 3. Counting] I. Title.
PZ7.K55740n 1984   [E]   84-27288
ISBN 0-688-05784-5